I Am Honest

Katie Peters

GRL Consultants,
Diane Craig and Monica Marx,
Certified Literacy Specialists

Pull Ahead Readers
People Smarts

Lerner Publications ◆ Minneapolis

Note from a GRL Consultant
This Pull Ahead leveled book has been carefully designed for beginning readers. A team of guided reading literacy experts has reviewed and leveled the book to ensure readers pull ahead and experience success.

Lerner Publications Company
An imprint of Lerner Publishing Group, Inc.
241 First Avenue North
Minneapolis, MN 55401 USA

For reading levels and more information, look up this title at www.lernerbooks.com.

Main body text set in Memphis Pro 24/39
Typeface provided by Linotype.

Photo Acknowledgments
The images in this book are used with the permission of: © Denise Andersen/Shutterstock Images, pp. 14, 15; © energyy/Getty Images, pp. 6, 7; © FamVeld/Shutterstock Images, pp. 10, 11, 16 (hat); © Figure8Photos/Getty Images, pp. 4, 5, 16 (blankets); © monkeybusinessimages/Getty Images, pp. 8, 9, 16 (sandwich); © PR Image Factory/Shutterstock Images, pp. 12, 13; © Sharomka/Shutterstock Images, p. 3.

Front cover: © michaeljung/Shutterstock Images

Library of Congress Cataloging-in-Publication Data

Names: Peters, Katie, author.
Title: I am honest / Katie Peters.
Description: Minneapolis, MN : Lerner Publications, 2022. | Series: Character builders (pull ahead readers people smarts—nonfiction) | Includes index. | Audience: Ages 4–7 | Audience: Grades K–1 | Summary: "Being honest is a sign of good character, and being honest feels good. Explore scenarios where honesty comes into play in everyday life. Pairs with the fiction title Ready for Bed"— Provided by publisher.
Identifiers: LCCN 2020015919 (print) | LCCN 2020015920 (ebook) | ISBN 9781728403526 (library binding) | ISBN 9781728423319 (paperback) | ISBN 9781728417813 (ebook)
Subjects: LCSH: Honesty—Juvenile literature.
Classification: LCC BJ1533.H7 P48 2021 (print) | LCC BJ1533.H7 (ebook) | DDC 179/.9—dc23

LC record available at https://lccn.loc.gov/2020015919
LC ebook record available at https://lccn.loc.gov/2020015920

Manufactured in the United States of America
2-1009212-48890-2/1/2023

Table of Contents

I Am Honest

Mom asked if I cleaned
my room today.
I said that I did.

Mom asked if I broke my toy. I said that I did.

Dad asked if I ate all of my lunch. I said that I did.

Dad asked if I lost
my mittens in the snow.
I said that I did.

Mom asked if I did
all of my homework.
I said that I did.

I feel good when
I tell the truth.

How do you feel when you tell the truth?

Did You See It?

blankets

hat

sandwich

Index